Juice of the lemon

Simone Mansell Broome

Published in 2008 by YouWriteOn.com
Copyright © Text Simone Mansell Broome
Copyright © Cover photo Jupiterimages
First Edition

The author asserts the moral right under the Copyright, Designs and Patents Act 1988 to be identified as the author of this work.

All Rights reserved. No part of this publication may be reproduced, stored in a retrieval system, or transmitted, in any form or by any means without the prior written consent of the author, nor be otherwise circulated in any form of binding or cover other than that in which it is published and without a similar condition being imposed on the subsequent purchaser.

Published by YouWriteOn.com

Contents

Earth — 5

Sherbet lemons...5
Domestic goddess..6
Seashells and a ra-ra skirt...7
Waiting, (England, early seventeenth century)...............8
Anniversary..9
Cub in the camp...10
No, not Mary Poppins..11
Look at them..12
Crocodile shoes..13
Tonight...14
Chinese lanterns, (released on my son's wedding day)...15
Gizmo R.I.P..16
Co-op..17
The house..18
Genie...20

Air — 21

Unwanted attentions..21
Jennifer's daddy..22
Convalescing..23
On meeting the locals..24
Prudence at Reid's Hotel...25
In praise of preparation...26

Avocado 27
Ode to Mister Fox 28
Manticipation 29
Missing dinner in Islamabad 30
On this morning 31
It's the thought that counts 32
Winter sky 33
Nobody's fool 34
The photo 36

Water — 37

Lullaby 37
Wetsuit 38
Missed call 39
Skin poem (or Here comes the science!) 40
Just desserts 42
Hot water bottle 43
Pixie boots 44
Earth and water 45
Mole 46
Kittens at tea 47
The movement of air 48
Mishap 49
My ex 50
High winds 52
Running away 53
Casablanca 54

Earth

Sherbet lemons

Carrying you I yearned for sherbet lemons:
sticky suspense, then splitting them open,
poking my tongue around and inside,
sucking out lemon dust, their acid burst
prickling my waiting mouth.

When the bag, brown or white, was empty,
I'd turn it inside out, check
for tell-tale broken lemon specks,
lick the paper wet. As I grew larger
I'd send him out for more. He'd scour the streets

at midnight, drain fleapit kiosks dry.
When asked, he'd shrug, say...it was
no big deal, that your grandmother
had eaten coal. By next time,
I was too tired for midnight cravings.

Domestic goddess

They send her, four feet seven of bone and sinew,
more muscled than I'd thought possible, and that mouth,
– me still stitched and silent, unable to stand upright,

hormones elbowing for attention. At first, she unnerves me,
doesn't mince her words; she spits them out, exhaling
bleach and brimstone, and whatever comes cheapest

in a pack of ten. Cleaning's her obsession; she likes things nice,
doesn't sit down, has no time for males – *good for one thing only
and no bloody use at that* – never happier

than with mop and pail, or doing battle with a steam iron,
forked tongue flickering; primed for the next skirmish.
I'd strip the clothes off their backs to wash them, she says,
if I ran out of things to do...

sluicing through the grime and dust, one-on-one
with dirt and mess, rumbling about the grubbiness
of men, the inevitability of soiled linen.

Seashells and a ra-ra skirt

You stir early, fretting:
a frill's unwound itself from an orange
ra-ra skirt, not to mention the tear
in red tartan,

both with shirred waists, the skirts
of a small skipping girl: you have to repair
them, make them good; have to do it by hand,
badly, slowly,

you can't use a machine,
so you let your eyes close, go find the dream,
take up your thread and sew, sew, the child
a blur of pink,

a raspberry tee-shirt,
white knickers with a seashell band, picked out
in cerise. *Hurry*, she's saying, *I can't
play out like this,*

and we've moved on to Sherwood
Forest, or Cinders' kitchen; you're dresser
to the star you'll always know she should be;
there are beads and shells,

real shells, attached
to the jaggedy hem of a dress you're trying
to do something with, cursing the fragility
of thread as you must

be done by morning.

Waiting, *(England, early seventeenth century).*

Today the household's busy, makes no sound; all know
what they have to do and do it well. No need for me
to chide or check their work. They bake, sew, sweep, keep
glances locked on women's tasks, silently, downcast.

Needles are threaded; lace collars re-attached
To the slender necks of shirts; linen and hose thrashed
dry on makeshift scaffolds in the yard; bitter winds
whip and sting our eyes, or we could say that this is so.

I am not obliged to speak; free for images
to fill my vigil – hair, thick and curly, bonny
as a girl's...two lads, their laughter curling up from
orchard to the house, playing secret games in tree

or field or wood, and a glimpse again, walking away,
a lively gait, their limbs still angular, swinging
swords, their grandfather's, *too large for them in truth*,
heads close, minds closer, off to practise being men..

There was a moment, (*my women had brought me stuff
to eat or drink, some cups, maybe broth, a drop of
honey on my lips*), a moment caught before dusk
fell, when I knew, felt, tasted they were lost. *I must*

bear this, I breathed, then madness licked about my feet,
leapt up, spilt over through the watchful house, out
into stables, dairy, courtyard, down across garden
to orchard and meadow, burning all to nothing.

Tomorrow night my husband will return; no need
for him to say that they are dead; no need to beg
forgiveness but he will. He will be grey, grey, aged
from his ride to London and back, failure writ in

ashes on his face. Bloodlust's a hungry mistress
who will not be denied. And our boys condemned, gone.
A cold winter is foretold. I may lose him too
to fever. I'll hold his hand, be still, count what's lost.

Anniversary

Never far from sequinned sea, from sky that hurts your eyes,
for hours you five, crushed into a car you didn't expect
to start, have bumped down rutted paths and dusty lanes,
seeing donkeys, large birds you can't quite name and a lone,
unexplained tortoise. It's been a rambling messy kind of day:

you gave up early on official sights, the rep's suggestions,
the bossiness of guide book, content just to explore, you've
got lost, overcharged and overheated but no one's
made a fuss, though now the postcard sunset, special meal,
well they've been snatched away – a child's fall, the sharp need

to find a sandy phrasebook buried at the bottom
of a rucksack, for town, doctor, stitches, iodine,
to mend a tear, put your day back on track.

Cub in the camp

We had to do a project, ask questions...
what did your Grandpa do in the war? Well, mine

was in Africa and he was given
a lion cub – pretty cool really. Don't ask

me why: something to do with Swahili, with
sending messages; doesn't make any sense

to me – I mean they were a long way
from Germany, right...If you don't believe me,

I'll show you – I've got the proof in black-and-white -–
that's all they could do then Miss, isn't it?

And he's playing with it; he's got his hand
In its mouth, is smiling, wearing uniform.

It's hard to believe he was ever that young,
but a present like that, I mean it's not just

for Christmas. Didn't anyone think it would grow?
Or what would happen when it got too big,

too playful? How would it cope back in the wild,
and I don't just mean other lions? This was

a war, right? Guns, tanks...but I guess if people
got used to killing other people, then

they wouldn't be fussed about just one lion.

No, not Mary Poppins

No, not Mary Poppins, not a carpetbag carrier,
a topnotch problem-solver, sorter and mender
of people, love, broken stuff, a seer-through
to the end of the heart of the matter, a spotter
of rainbows.

But it's a close-run thing. Sure, we have never *seen*
her talk to that parrot; never seen her fly or ascend
the stairs by banister; but we've shrieked *a handbag*
in our shrillest Lady Bracknell tones as we've watched
her pull out

from the bowels of that shabby bag, the only bag
we've ever known her to own, all sorts of emergency
equipment, improbable essentials, from hair bobbles
to spare knickers for small people, tights for ladders, from
shoe polish

and safety pins to fuses, aspirins, tow ropes, kitchen sinks,
cartons of drinks and mugs and bowls that fold away
for thirsty dogs and tots, and paperbacks with no backs
stuffed with jokes about elephants and penguins
and custard

for queues and jams and tantrums we mustn't let happen;
things for fixing it, for making do, those pick-us-ups
and get-us-throughs. We've seen her turn up in a puff
of smiles, flushed with exertion, her face streaked,
smudged with dirt -

it could be soot - she's brought that bag of tricks,
and a picnic, her gifts of practical magic.

Look at them

Look at them, she said. *I must have been at least
a C then*; and I had to admit that in the pic of her
and her penultimate ex – she was rounder, more
womanly, with firm, high breasts. And each time
she went back to him, they grew again. He was,
most definitely, looking for a mum.

Now we scramble through the box, fumbling
for snaps of her with the most recently departed -
And yes, it's true. No boobs, a catwalk shape,
that size zero so much discussed of late.
But then he was a legs and bum man. I concur...
it's a mystery to us how her shape's morphed

to fit their fantasies. I scan the current suitors
in my head. She says *I think they're growing again.*
We watch her bloom – a century, a clock
of lion's teeth's blown on one breath,
on a young woman's **yes**, dissolving in laughter,
in wanting just to please.

Crocodile shoes

There are crocodile shoes on the doormat, pointy
and swirly, rather larger than I'm used to seeing.
At least an 11.The thought crosses my mind briefly,
about some correlation between size-of-feet and...

but maybe it was noses, and this guy, owner of large, alien,
decorated shoes, has a rather squat, squashed nose,
not bent, but neither elegant nor cute, and he
is a house guest I've stumbled across this morning.

I would have preferred it if he'd followed type, been bleary,
incoherent, mumbled a bit while trying to remember
his manners, but this chap crushes my hand, bounces,
noisily, around my kitchen, keeps talking, full of smarm

and blarney, sings too, when outside, with a repertoire
of the rugby and sea shanty type, rather lewd in a trad
sort of way; wears wraparound shades indoors,
is, (or so I'm told, in a loud stage whisper), a black belt

somethingorotherDan in all sorts of martial arts,
and, when not sleeping in my spare bedroom,
choreographs fights for action movies – the sort
that won't get nominated for awards, aren't blockbusters,

but nonetheless earn a tidy sum, have a loyal following
amongst the testosterone-rich...Be that as it may,
he's cooking bacon, smiling too much, and I can't help
staring at his crocodile shoes.

Tonight

I am earth mother Aga-diva I am DeliaNigella
I am everywoman who smiles sage and
enigma from the cover of a much-smeared tome
I am conjurer of small culinary miracles

since the simple and the joyously normal
are things rarely possible to engineer I've
downed and refilled my generous glass of
white dusted floury hands against my skirt

brushed ample hips against the warmth of
an oven felt achieved absurd as the things I
have created the products of my domestic
aspirations will all be gone within two days I

would like it to be said by way of epitaph that
though I never really mastered pastry and
though my meringues left a lot to be desired I
could whip up something ok from almost zilch

and I showed a certain stylistic flair even as
sous-chef or kitchen maid and that while I was
often sadly lacking in loftier spheres and
very definitely had feet of earthenware I did

just once or twice make marvels happen.

Chinese lanterns, (released on my son's wedding day).

Look at it in a cardboard box, flown in on metal wings
from half a world away, folded on itself,
the thinnest of paper concertinas, the flimsiest of ribs:
this framework gives no hint of its promise.

This evening, we'll hold up lanterns, let them belly with air,
feel them tugging against us, let them go.
We'll have no control; they could be trapped in branches,
torn by thorns. They could be blown for miles.

Tonight we'll sack the matchmakers; you are ready
for this launching, filled with our hopes, your love.

They are more than the sum of their fragile parts;
let's watch them fly.

Gizmo R.I.P.

On the day after my birthday
Gizmo was cremated. I know
this to be a fact. On the gate
that leads into Green Castle Woods,

before you get to choosing which dots,
which coloured route to pick, paper
pinned to the post tells us his name,
the date, how he was disposed of,

not laid to rest in soft earth, not
decaying like these crab apples
at my feet, the first windblown leaves
I scuffle. 'Summerleaze' officialdom,

one D S Williams, has signed this
certificate in rounded hand.
Are Gizmo's ashes scattered here?
What's in a name? I picture

a cheerful mutt with undecided
ears – up, down or badly folded –
was this a favoured spot for runs
and rootling through the brambles?

Nothing else is certain. He's dead,
burnt but did this document drop
from a pocket or a bag, is it
waiting for his former owner

to come back – perhaps distracted
now by puppy or by a child –
or is this card like the brass plaque
on the weathered bench at the brow

of the hill...*in memory of...*
he loved these woods, this place, this view...?

Co-op

I'm not sure how we got them
or how we proved our need
for fourteen milk tokens, Co-op milk tokens,
each week.

Gambling chips or board game counters,
we'd neatly stack them
under empties, confident
of pre-dawn

doorstep swaps by silent milkmen,
and of those streetwise
streetcorner magpies picking on
some other victims.

The house

It's out of your way. You 're on a hunt for paint,
a whim that's hit you when the usual d-i-y is shut.
You drive past. Strange how little you remember

but a child would have painted it something
like this. A square house, tile-hung, redbricked,
a mirror image of itself, with two chimneys,
small, white-paned windows,
and a door aproned in quarry tiles,
topped by some sort of porch – a nun's headdress -
but a nun from a modern order.

It's marooned inside tall hedges, dark
and evergreen, with a laburnum,
showy and unexpected, in the front lawn –

no, too small for lawn.
It's become perfect, solid and substantial,
an unspoilt version of itself, the stuff of dreams
for a postmodernist, debt-embracing family.
It's quaint but not Cadbury's,
in a vibrant community… good motorway links
and an assortment of upmarket eateries.

You hated it then, too far from the village heart,
those blessings of church and rectory,
neither smart enough nor old enough,

unthatched, unmullioned, ungravelled,
unmodconned, ticking none of your schoolmates'
boxes. You look again. You see its honest charms:
tastes change. Someone's taking
good care of it, and now you wonder
if the swing is still there.

Genie

We only ever finish a house
just as we're leaving. We move from project
to project. This one follows type – I gain
a kitchen as the boards go up – a kitchen such
as dreams are made of, magazines sold - warm
and buttery, welcoming...but, spoilt by that view,

the flower bed beneath the window, filled
as it is with red-hot-pokers, forgotten toys,
weeds, all the debris of family life. We dig
it over, toil one clammy Autumn afternoon,
bury bulbs we'll not be there to see,
but find a ribbed, emerald green bottle.

I wash it, line it up with others on a sill
where light plays through. And then the dreams
begin, whisperings and murmurings, brushings
past on stairs, and calling out our names,
but the room is always empty. *We've let him out,*
my daughter says, *released him; he's like*

the genie of this house. And so, with everything
packed tight and engines running, on the move
again, we both shout **stop**, and with the only tool
to hand, a tarnished tablespoon, we dig
a glass-bottle-sized hole,
and put that genie back.

Air

Unwanted attentions

I was taught to be kind,
to divert and distract,
to politely decline,
to turn down gently, with tact.

It's nice to be wanted
and flattery's fine,
but your ardour's undented,
and you can't read the signs.

You don't seem to do rejected;
softly seems to light your fire.
You don't seem at all deflected;
translate 'no' as wild desire.

I'm not weak at the knees;
I won't melt at your touch;
I'm glad that I please
but this is really too much.

Jennifer's daddy

Jennifer's daddy has a hobby.
Jennifer's daddy walks late every afternoon
to the end of a manicured lawn,

and he opens the door of a small dollshouse workshop,
enters and shuts it. Inside he paints,
with precision and delicacy,

not for display or for sale. Just because.
And Jennifer's daddy has a long, pale face and sparse,
pale hair, and nothing about him

is clear or memorable, but neither
does it jar. Jennifer's mummy is solid and square,
has a face that's seen too much

weather, a face with lumps and bumps. She makes
paper-thin sandwiches without crusts.
Jennifer, who favours the maternal line,

turns up blotchy, rumpled one morning after
an *unnamed* bug. Rumours puddle our gossip-starved
yard. Jennifer's daddy, it's said,

crossed the dewdamp grass to his shed, collected
his painted gnomes, fled to live with his ballet dancer lover,
somewhere far more glamorous than here.

Convalescing

On the mend again she'd take you out, make
you wrap up warm, *blow those cobwebs away:
let's stretch those legs, put roses in those cheeks,
trot round the block.* In fact, there was no block;
you'd be out for an hour, or maybe more,
walking past where your old school once had been,

past shrinking fields grazed by red brick boxes
breeding fast beyond the college - *being
built for teachers* she said. Past the new vets
you took your cat and dog to. You'd talk or
she would - you working out you didn't want
to be a vet - just as well since sometimes

animals, like your cousin, didn't get
better. Sometimes you had to help them die.
Perhaps you'd be an actress or writer,
as nothing else seemed possible; and this
the winter after the winter of snows
that lay banked by hedges, frosted

laurel, when birds quite literally dropped
from perches, when some *crazed* person poisoned
pets - poisoned one of yours - bodies frozen,
undiscovered, till the thaw. *This is beyond
your understanding.* For now, this winter,
it's enough that you get better, keep warm.

On meeting the locals

You've forgotten the hairiness, moustaches like
zealous freedom fighters, that threat
of all-over growth, of hair creeping down to meet
the hair on back –

he was a swimmer and he said that's what they did -
waxing of backs to boost the slip
and glide through water…out of his element you
found him slippery.

From the window of a Fiat Panda an arm
extends, clutching a crook, banging
it against car, against tarmac, against earth.
He calls and whistles

at sheep and goats who are unmoved, zigzagging
up the road ahead of him: his other hand's
shared between wheel and cigarette. You note again
the cottonbud thinness

of their legs, their shagpile coats… hear the line
in your head about sheep and goats
and telling them apart. There's little chance
of a friendly word; you're staying, after all,

with people who once dared to feed his cats.
The air is heavy with wild sage, salt,
bougainvillea. And bells, their metallic echoing song,
you've forgotten them too.

Prudence at Reid's Hotel

Lady Prudence Jellicoe casts herself
from a terrace at Reid's Hotel: you've seen it

while surfing, now net it illicitly cased in glass
down some plush carpeted corridor –

Daily Sketch maybe – (you've strayed off piste
from your 3.00pm date with tiered iced fancies,

miniature crustless sandwiches rolled so thin,
to scrape up what's left of the twenties, the thirties,

to breathe in some authentic flavour). You're told
she only learned to dive that trip – Prudence playing

swallow, poised above the Atlantic, boylike woman
severe and stylish, slender as a Zelda or a Daisy,

conquistador of elements, no mere simpering soubrette.
You return to the many pixels of Dixons' finest

flashing amongst silver plate, Madeira cake,
starched white linen.

In praise of preparation

Though passion is smashing, preparation is all.
It would have been nice to have known your intentions;
I'd like to have looked at my best.

And if you'd only alluded
to your quest to denude me,
then I'd have factored in buffing and grooming,

or at least added a measure
of graft to my endeavours,
to my plan to look better undressed.

Au naturel may be swell but
past your teens - tricky as hell,
and if you deny this, you're lying or dreaming.

It would have been nice to have known you were scheming,
that my seduction was looming...
if I must be undone or won, an early warning's my request.....

Spontaneity's over-rated!
Quite frankly I hate it,
and though passion may be smashing, preparation is all.

Avocado

Pick me;
pick me up, cradle me, inky dark in your waiting palm,
my body tilting to the flicker of a pulse at your wrist,
my head grazing your curled fingertips,
me steadied by your thumb.

Don't bruise me;
Don't assume resilience if my flesh gives in
to your pressure: my pitted skin will still mark
if you are harsh – do not cut me until the moment
too is ripe, then slice me,

spread my halves,
part these twin vessels, moist yet minutes from
greying, don't forget that ticking clock, fill me with
some ready concoction of oil, of wine gone sour,
that you made earlier.

Ode to Mister Fox

Wow! Your fabled tail, your lustrous bustling bushy tail,
it struts the questions – *am I fabulous, am I fantastic?*
Are you hell? Now I'm in thrall

to that pelt, the scrumptious sweep of your back, the swell
of your russet chest rising up to that strong neck,
such long yellow teeth, those gold sleepy eyes,

neat feet, fleetfooted, hold on...I can't wait!
I'm in hock to the shock of that dark musky scent,
sexy and bosky, promising plenty:

I'm disarmed by your sangfroid,
your *je ne sais quoi*. One flickering look, one flare
of white and I'm snared somehow;

hooked by that smell, that tail, those tawny charms,
I'll be your flame, your vixen, doxy...
Oh foxy my foxy!.

Manticipation

Oh manopause, man of many pauses,
you are in training for tonight's big game.

Green bottles have been chosen, arranged, chilled;
a space has been created on the couch,

pets and papers brushed aside. The remote
has been uncovered, dusted, placed in waiting,

your digits primed for action. The Screwfix
catalogue has been abandoned, unread,

and I am once more obliged to take my fix
of sorting socks for satisfaction, have

an early night, charge up those batteries
and find some thoughts to think outside

the blue sky of that box.

Missing dinner in Islamabad.

Of course he knows something has happened,
bow tie knotted to perfection,
the noise is eerie, loud like nothing
he's ever heard, but then the stillness

filled with smoke chills him more. He stumbles
back, thin dinner jacket speckled
with warm flecks, to the company Merc,
feels for his key fob, is consoled

by the beep, protects the mirror shine
of those shoes, sidesteps a dark pool
spreading at the kerb edge, and a hand
half clenches, uncurls. He retches,

feels for the passenger side, climbs in, across,
drives through the starstripped night,
his meal forgotten, unable to shut out
that disconnected hand.

On this morning

On this morning ,
a boy crouches in red earth drawing
with a pointed stone,

two children stand
at the base of a tree, looking up. A third
disentangles a kite:

the air is perfumed,
sweet and weighty. One hundred and seventy
million people wait.

This is the third day
of mourning. Swift burial, swift grieving. When
she died, it was all

so rushed...she could have been
anybody's, *any body*, a granite day, not
this day, hazy,

the scented breath
of a continent, kites fluttering, petals
powdered with hot dust.

It's the thought that counts...

Only a flashback, late November in Dusseldorf,
a weekend when neither of you had expected to be
so cold, your noses pressed to misted windows, and two things

jumped out at you, a wardrobe, waxed, ornately carved, much
cheaper, more desirable than those you'd looked at back home,
(but you quashed that want with practical considerations,

Lufthansa might object,) and a picture made of wine corks,
more a noticeboard. Somehow this picture comes back to you,
hand-in-hand with the old chestnut, *let's just make our presents*

*this year, let's do homespun, let's dig deep, let's rediscover
a purer Yule*. A couple of design tweaks. You decide
yours will stand or lie in rows behind glass, deep frames you find

knocked down in Habitat. Much virtuous cork collection
later, hours of arranging and rearranging and it's
almost December; thus far you've made two, and you're so
pleased

with the fruits of your labours that you decide to keep these
for your own kitchen, the smaller frame filled with indigo
ink printed ferrules of cork from champagne, sparkling white

or rose, cava, anything with fizz, the larger with rows
of wine corks, packed sausage-tight, the end result delightful...
You still have frames to spare, you plan to make more as Christmas

gifts, but disappointment strikes a bitter advent blow. On
closer scrutiny, could this scheme be honestly seen as
fulfilling your dreams of a simpler, more authentic, less

commercial festival...and could you possibly empty,
for each present, between now and Christmas, one hundred and
twelve wine bottles, (*one hundred and forty four of bubbly*)?

Winter sky

They came out once a year, cardboard coffins
of candied fruits, mandarin, lime, lemon,
clear-lidded, all-the-better-for-seeing
their alien, citrus sweetness. Only
at Christmas. They just turned up with the dates
and figs, plastic two-tined fork included.

Excited whispers that there would be gifts;
there was more to come, that, even as you
feasted, wise men might be trudging towards
you from somewhere out East. A half-circle
of sugared lemon hangs up there tonight;
guide for gift-bearers, beacon in the black.

Nobody's fool

Love you he said
whenever he caught her cautious look
or she was silent for a while
and love's his barbed and baited hook
sheathed with a jaunty sporting smile

Love you he said
lids lowered signalling tender sad
*how can I know this'll be better
understand me – I've been so bad*
every phrase a velvet fetter

Love you he said
as he explains why he failed to show
too cold too dark too wet too ill
and yes she feels she should know
better but she's sympathetic still

Love you he said
low voice so hungry with persuasion
an anniversary unremembered
she's aware he's not quite craven
enough but for now her doubt's dismembered

Love you he said
*can't find my i-Pod and I'm so tired
I don't deserve this love you feel*
she fears his credit's long expired
that she's holding on to empty thrills

Love you he said
it's so hard to choose between two wives
once more emptying out those loins
if I could be granted two lives -
tough call for our hero – a coin

will be tossed something will be lost
loved you she said .

The photo

There is a photo
taken in the NEC,
back view of a younger, longer-haired me,
arms and legs clasped tight around my body
and they are the arms and legs of a balloon,
a cuddling greetings balloon
from a balloon exhibition
at the NEC.

We were there to tempt us, persuade us
to invest in a venture. The photo
was to remind us later
how delightful it would be
for a loved one to open a box,
and for a longlimbed balloon to leap out
and embrace him or her.
We were unmoved. In fact not at all tempted.

I remember other limbs wound
tight around my torso,
helping hands unpeeling him, arm by arm,
leg by leg, re-attaching him to the body
of a waiting helper. The process needing to be quick
and clean, or he'd reverse it instantly, clinging
to me with mucus-laden sobs.
I'd run way and not look back,
my shoulders wet, my eyes damp too.

Water

Lullaby

People say I'm a good mother, no way
one of those shakers. It would've taken
a helluva lot to make me lay a
finger on one of those kids. Such a small

shove it was, wouldn't have left a mark. No
harm meant. Go to sleep, go to sleep, go to
sleep. We were just full of food and yes, some
wine, slicing a little grown-up time. It

was happy hour till midnight. But she fell -
wouldn't have hurt at home, Granny next door,
soft, carpeted floors. Metal and marble
and tiles in this bloody flat...bloody floor...

what can you do about bleeding? It was
ev'rywhere, splashing and spurting. My hands.
Her hair. That noise. Something to mop it up,
make it stop, go away – okay, it was

the nearest thing, a pillow; it's what you'd
have grabbed to stem that flow. The others could
have stirred; there'd be no more playing, no more
twirly cocktail umbrellas...bloody floor,

bloody flat, bloody foreign – go to sleep,
go to sleep. It's happy hour till midnight.

Wetsuit

Hot stuff - enough to turn the sensible quite loopy!
Aerodynamic in neoprene, so streamlined, so sleek,
oh rubbersulted swain, I'll be your ardent groupie!

My cheeks they are quite flushed; my pulse is rather weak;
by the flapping of your flipflops, I feel so truly captivated:
aerodynamic in neoprene, so streamlined, so sleek.
Though men in well-cut leathers I can find 18-rated,
and I'm a sucker for the cuteness of some guys in shorts,
by the flapping of your flipflops, I feel so truly captivated.

Your IQ may be rippling, but I'm still tingling at the taut
contours of your muscles in your wetsuit so divine,
though I'm a sucker for the cuteness of you, clad in shorts.
•
Oh my damp and dishy dolphin, my flake, my 99,
I'm an avid admirer of your toned, your well-honed butt -
contours of your muscles in your wetsuit so divine.

Get primeval, down to basics, take me to your cave, your hut
hot stuff - enough to turn the sensible quite loopy!
I'm an avid admirer of your toned, your well-honed butt –
oh rubbersuited swain, I am your ardent groupie!

Missed call

Consider the moles in the grass –
now you can see where they've been,
so consider how much bigger

a spaceship is; surely if they were in the habit
of landing
in these leafy rural parts they'd leave
evidence, indentations, scorched ground,
which you'd notice on driving to work?

You'd nod knowingly – *Aaaah,
it's them - been busy , haven't they?*
Then again, why choose here? Think of fly-tipping,
and of local outrage at the use of our lane
as a rat-run. If they landed here

as a regular thing there'd be rumblings
about the noise and the light pollution which would
escalate into musterings
of resistance, and I'm inclined to think,
a letter of protest – *we the undersigned...*

and then, consider me, why me? Wouldn't you want
to snaffle a more standard specimen
of humanity? Now, do you really think
I'd be top of their hit list, a have-to-have,
and would you want the hassle
of picking me? No -

I wasn't abducted by aliens; I wasn't spirited away,
but I did forget
to ring you.

Skin poem (or Here comes the science!)

Gather round paranoid sisters – you all know who you are,
'cos the boffins from Boots have conjured an elixir in a jar -
magic for the complexion -
an answer to the tragic question that vexes women,
why a man's wrinkles are sexy crinkles and crow's feet
just mean he's smiled a lot, but laughter lines ain't funny for us,
so some turn back the clock with botox,
(not for those with phobias for needles or pain),
and we're seduced again into using confusing, line-reducing
lotions and potions called - Time Delay, Recapture -
but now, new hope, rapture…resurfacing not surgery,
and this solution's a sort of vitamin A dilution,
no nips, no tucks, no big bucks, no knife,
reclaim your youth, reclaim your life.

Think magic knickers, magic dress, to be found in that alchemist,
M & S; they'll lift you up and hold you in like a firm embrace;
now chemists have the formula for the same thing for your face.
Some of us read New Scientist; some look at dresses in Hello:
we know this stuff works cos Horizon says so.
No need to be cheated by genetics; no need to buy cosmetics
far beyond our means…
eight glasses of water, no sun, no booze, no nicotine,
and early nights! No, we want instant results;
we want excess; we want to get tight. So what if beauty's skin deep:
we want the facelift in a pot, we want the wrinkle-busting lot, not
our beauty sleep…and we want it now, anyhow.

Because we're worth it, in office, shop or bar, from near and from far,
we've a right to be beautiful; we've a right to be thin;
it's not vanity…it's save the world and save our skins,
and yeah, poverty – if it ain't history – then it sure as hell's a sin,

and those sweet little natives with their unique ingredients,
selected and collected from just beneath the jungle canopy,
I'm sure they're treated fairly, given Levis and a telly,
and if they get a bit bolshy, a McDonalds or a KFC
will be erected in the clearing where the forest used to be.

Nivea, Vaseline, Olay and Atrixo,
names our mums trusted to keep their skins just so,
but now it's a face-off, my sisters and what do bunnies know?
We want sexy, we don't want to think about what's in our creams,
and, in fact, if fat from bums is crucial for the serum,
bung it in…peptides and humectants,
boswelox and H2O, make me look much younger
but don't let my efforts show.

It's a killer, my darlings, forget the dermal filler;
acrylic fingernails in the dyke
because we all like to believe
we've found the portal to being immortal.
We have a right to be beautiful, we have a right to be thin,
and we're buffed up and trussed up and loved up
with the geeks from Boots and our deep deep throats
can be soothed and smoothed by the creams produced
by men in white coats, cos we're worth it, my sisters,
and who needs the truth,
when there's magic for 17 quid and that promise of youth.

Just desserts

No we
won't just slurp a latte
share a melted after eight
for once let's leave our points behind us
break out break free from calories
put a hex on that GI index
from strict diets let's just riot

Yes let's
do pudding let's cut loose
unnotch the belt forget the bulge
let's live a little indulge
dreamy steamy creamy juicy
awfully moreish chocolate moussey
is it true what they say about
chocolate

Yes let's
get passionate over passion cake
sizzling over drizzle cake
trysting through the trifle
lusting over ginger crust
tumbling in the crumble
spooning coulis round the tarte
sticky toffee…aaaah - banoffee
dip a berry in the fondue
bite that cherry

Yes let's
flick those fruity toppings from the tips of noses
get absorbed in mango sorbet
brule baby brule
focus now on feeding frenzy
in the mood for
rich dark tastes...chocolate chocolate...let's
do pudding

Hot water bottle

You see,
hot water bottles get cold my darling,
and here, on the cusp of a cloudrare,

starcrammed night,
a waning harvest moon and chilly dawn, mine,
(in threadworn blue teddybear suit),

belies its name.
I work it down to the gap between mattress
and bed end, toes on cramp warning,

my needs simple -
just you, radiating heat as you do,
igniting sparks, close-cuddling
me warm.

Pixie boots

I ask you what you can still picture...
pixie boots you say. You say I was wearing pixie boots
and that I took them off at the water's edge,
so we could paddle that grey October afternoon.

You say it was sunny; I remember a dull day,
neither stormy nor bright nor bitterly cold,
the sun just trying, now and then,
to break through and make a difference.

You talk of lunch – a chav caff – stewed tea
and jacket spuds with beans or cheese or both.
I'm going to make that be some other day. And
as for pixie boots, well I can see the heels,

but there's nothing too pointy or elvish, and I
had packed sensible footwear...we were just
in too much haste to reach that tired slice of shingle,
(only a breath snatched between tussock and graphite sea),

for me to change shoes first. You mention
the bleached wooden pallet, you licking and
sucking and drying my salty feet, both of us
blind to all dogwalkers beachcombers, passersby.

Let's agree on that flotsam pallet, the sand in my hair,
the kissing of toes. But I think the weather may've turned,
that perhaps we rushed back, ran for shelter,
spent a long slow afternoon listening to the rain.

Earth and water

At three am wakefulness can seem a judgement,
make you tearful.

Dry-eyed here, parched too, despite that tumbler
downed before bed, the one just after
two goblets of pinot grigio.

In darkness now, owlhoots and nameless
animal cries for company;
am at my uncle's funeral and before – whisky poured,

he turns to ask his wife of forty-four years
what's your poison, turns back, drops crumpled
to the floor. The ambulance man, a family friend,

blubs plump tears, says *it's a good death,
a good way to go*, that he'll be really much missed,
a glass-half-full bloke, whose face swims before me,

slightly misty, details coarsened, and then falls back.
So on, treading water, to where I've buried scraps
from the funeral. I peel back the feeling, recall

words said, readings, (yet not what was sung or played),
that they closed the rainwashed roads in that little town,
filled the chapel, filled the porch, trampled sodden grass

outside to hear his sending off broadcast, rippling out…
They'd come to pay or show respect, the size of the hole,
its shape and depth measurable in that place

he'd never left, would never leave. Had never seen the need.
It all fades like a wet-Sunday-afternoon film. You seep in;
you and thoughts of what we leave behind.

Mole

On sandworn steps we find him splayed
like a cartoon Felix, his body chocolate-dipped,
with sphinctery snout,
and the fingers of a bloodless pianist.

My dad caught moles. He collected them
in hessian sacks, was paid a penny for each
I think. It all gets muddled with the cold,
motherless farmhouse, no school bus,

the years before the war, and how I ought
to give thanks for what I had. Instead
I wanted more, wanted warmth,
for there to be something between

the silence and the sermon, and for a dad who
smiled, paid the bills, whose anger
wasn't bloodless.

Kittens at tea

Indigo Abednego, down you go, nice and slow.
Shadrach, Meshach, feline black,
can't look back. Let's observe proprieties –

table limbs all gingham-skirted, warm the pot,
real leaf tea. We'll call jam conserve.
Mother's fruitful - out they drop - indigo kittens,

us kids sitting, sitting. Hide them in a towel-lined box;
lick them, suckle them - too small, too blind
to pick up and cuddle them. Sandwiches in triangles

with no crusts, crumpets, scones and battenburg:
more for the water butt: litter all dead:
Fry's chocolate spread. Shadrach, Meshach, down you go

in a hessian sack - Abednego.

The movement of air

That sudden movement of air, small
but audible, like the rush or bubble
on releasing the pressure
of hot water bottle or flask, that pause.

No door banging here, just flapping
of rubber fins, swishing of skirted barriers,
squeaking of shoes, soft and rubber soled
on shiny see-your-face-in-them floors,

where all is moulded, mostly unbreakable,
the doors, the shoes, those stubborn wheels
on trollies bringing things, taking
stuff away, containers for bodily fluids,

tubes and phials, beakers, scrubs
and latex gloves. And the bed undulating,
voicing its marine language, relieving
some other pressures, while on board

there's motion sickness, a small
confused body falling into pillows,
mattress, linen; everything shrinking, even
those black button eyes. Vellum skin,

thinner by the minute. You pat cream
into wrists tiny as a five year old's,
tentative, unsure as that first kiss
on a newborn's fontanelle.

Mishap

Sense it before he comes in, heat
hangs heavy this late late April
afternoon. The engine cuts, stops,
sky parenthisised by jumbos,

press second teabag against side
of a mug, flick to join the first
in a ceramic ramekin,
pour in milk, your throat tightening;

he lifts his hand and you notice
what's missing, find an ice-cream tub
plus lid, plastic ice tray thumped on
worktop edge, cubes, splinters skitter

across the tiles, run down the path,
sink to your knees by oil drip tray,
scrabble in oil, in gravel for
severed digits, scoop them into

their Tupperware bed…back to skid
on floor, find phone, (on door, white goods,
walls, there are streaks, splashes), had you
dreamt this, there would have been less blood.

My ex

No, not hanging there, nor even my last –
much water under bridges since and yes,
I did that poem, knew it off by heart.
They said I'd a natural gift...you see,
things came so easily – Mum's golden boy:
I was lucky, couldn't put a foot wrong:
it made my sister spit. Never saw much
of the old man though. Back to the ex then,

she's at the back in Jacques Vert, strappy shoes –
unflattering to those chunky ankles.
Not aged well. Best girl around she was – once.
Bound to be mine. Peaches and cream like some...
beauty queen, but not much up top. Should've
run when I got back but her mum was dead
set on it – the works, the whole caboodle.
She'd bought her hat; had a soft spot for me,

but I had a way with older women.
Turned to fat now, both of them. You could see
she would. Take away the Del Monte and
the Fussells, that Elnetted bright barnet –
nothing. No sculpted bones, no class, and not
even half the lights switched on. I took her
places she'd never have gone, but she was
out-of-place, missing home, missing her mum.

Not exactly hands on as dad...we weren't
back then, but I was a good provider.
Stayed out, stayed away. She cried far too much.
That's my younger one, bright lad, no thanks to
his mother. His bride's clever too, but sharp,
a bit too sharp for my liking. Doesn't laugh
at my jokes. Party animal, that's me.
I could see she was lonely, perceptive

I was, didn't miss a trick; didn't want
another, thought two was plenty, but found
myself hoping for a girl, pictured her
blonde, not dim but not so difficult, less
inclined to moaning and groaning. A boy.
She even got that wrong. If they hadn't
had to wrap it, take it, we might have made
this work, but she turned her face away, turned

to the wall. I patted her cold shoulder –
there was no consolation. When she stopped
weeping, first it was the sherry and then
she hit on some younger bloke, flung herself
at him, said he understood. Since that day
in the hospital I'd played away, found
comfort elsewhere. Our bed was frosty.
You bet it didn't last. I was a hard act
to follow. Yes, that's the Duchess, half cut,
looking rough, showing her bra strap. You'd think
she'd drag herself together - for today.

High winds

From my sheets I can see there's too much wind
in these trees. They're thrashing and kicking,
insisting I notice, flexing to the
rim of no return. Snapping point. *Do not*

say you sailed today. Have I confessed this
yet? Add wind to that list of the things
I fear. My berth's narrower; I keep it
trim. If the chart warns me of dragons, I

steer clear. Me in my brass-ended bed, in
the high-ceilinged room – such a bed, such a
room as I've dreamed of…in a house in a
place I've been stumbling towards forever.

And you not here. Tell me you just went to
look at your little boat, patted her flank,

got blown home.

Running away

You can see I was serious. I was even
thinking about how many pairs and which
shoes to pack, mindful that you do
not see me as a flatties kind of girl.

But heels, high heels, were not invented for
the swift exit, and elopement over
cobbles could be lethal in slingbacks. Yet
I digress. At this point, I'd like to say

my intentions were sincere...that you were
this close to taking me away, making
a dishonest woman of me here. I
had even changed the blade on my razor,

counted out my vitamins, enough to last the
next few weeks, found some old film canister
thing to stick them in...ticking stuff off on
my list. I change my mind, backtrack, rewind

at no return - *it is my right* – do not
call me contrary for being wary.
There has been a shift of emphasis. The
air is thickly perfumed with *butyousaids*

and *thoughtyoumeants*, with shrinking forevers,
as we step back, unpack those bags, slip from
frisson to swansong, from a risky maybe
to a no-not-a-cat-in-hell's-chance-never.

Casablanca

Change all the locks;
throw away the keys.
You wanted Ingrid;
but I'm afraid you've got me.

I'm just treading water,
not drowning but waving;
I know what I oughtta -
no, I ain't misbehavin'.

Nailed flag to his mast
in penultimate frame,
now rewinding the past
and its intimate games;

cos the fat lady's hoarse -
can't hold out for long;
Ingrid's banished of course
and they're playing *our song*.

Acknowledgements

Some of these poems have appeared in Carillon, Envoi and Roundyhouse magazines. Others have been shortlisted in competitions and have appeared in anthologies – Buzz, Cinnamon Press and Ragged Raven.

The encouragement of members of Acorns and Teifi Scribblers is gratefully recorded here.

Thanks to Roger for layout and artwork and much practical assistance.